First Class
Written by Tommy Watkins
AF481029

I'm at the airport, catching a flight home to Chicago.

I upgraded my ticket to a First-Class ticket. Tonight, I'm flying in style.

I received access to a magical lounge with my First-Class ticket. This lounge has food, drinks, and even a shower!

I freshen up with a shower and indulg myself through the buffet.

After eating, I received a text from the airline that there is a computer glitch i the system. My flight was delayed si, hours!

There's nothing to do now except keep drinking while I wait for my flight.

Another hour passed, and I received another text that my flight was cancel. because of a computer glitch.

I approach the flight concierge in the lounge. How am I going to get home?

This lounge is not only filled with foo.
drinks, and relaxation, it grants you
one wish to make your travel experienc
great. I wish to get on the first flight
back home.

A plane arrives at the gate, ready to tak
off. I sit in my first-class seat, ready t
take off, up in the night sky,

back home to Chicago.

The End